PRINCESS of PETS

The Cuddly Seal

Paula Harrison

Illustrated by
Olivia Chin Mueller

nosy
crow

For Jacob and Samuel

First published in the UK in 2020 by Nosy Crow Ltd
The Crow's Nest, 14 Baden Place,
Crosby Row, London SE1 1YW

www.nosycrow.com

ISBN: 978 1 78800 673 6

Nosy Crow and associated logos are trademarks and/or registered
trademarks of Nosy Crow Ltd

Text copyright © Paula Harrison, 2020
Illustrations © Olivia Chin Mueller, 2020

The right of Paula Harrison and Olivia Chin Mueller to be identified as
the author and illustrator respectively of this work has been asserted.
All rights reserved

A CIP catalogue record for this book is available from the British Library

Printed and bound in the UK by Clays Ltd, Elcograf S.p.A.

Papers used by Nosy Crow are made from wood grown in
sustainable forests.

1 3 5 7 9 10 8 6 4 2

Chapter One

A Day by the Sea

Bea skipped down the beach with a picnic basket in one hand and a bucket in the other. It was a perfect summer's day and seagulls were circling around the fishing boats as they chugged across the sparkling sea into the harbour. A warm breeze swept across the bay, lifting Bea's hair and making the waves dance.

"Come back, Bea!" yelled Natasha,

Bea's older sister. "We don't want to eat the picnic so close to the water. We'll get soaked when the tide comes in."

Bea dug her toes into the warm sand. She couldn't wait to go swimming with Keira, her best friend, who had joined them for the day. They had all set off from Ruby Palace with their buckets and spades and their swimming towels, accompanied by Nancy, one of the palace maids.

Bea was the middle one of the three royal children. Alfie, her little brother, had been bouncing around the palace with his fishing net since six o' clock that morning. Bea wasn't surprised that their dad, King George, had looked so relieved as he waved them off from the front steps. He'd glanced at Bea sternly just before they left. "Remember, Beatrice!

No bringing home stray dogs or cats or hamsters. In fact, don't pick up anything furry at all!"

Bea had pulled a face. Everyone knew she was animal mad. She was always on the lookout for animals that needed her help and she had already rescued a kitten and a puppy, as well as a tiny reindeer called Marshmallow. Each time she rescued an animal the king would say, "Beatrice, the palace is no place for a pet!" But Bea knew in her heart that she would never be able to resist a creature in trouble.

"Hurry up, Bea!" Natasha shouted. "Alfie says he's hungry."

"All right – I'm coming!" Bea swung the basket as she walked back up the beach.

Natasha began laying out the picnic

rug. Keira helped Bea to unpack all the rolls and cakes, and the big bottle of lemonade. "My mum and dad sent some food too." She unzipped a large lunch bag. "There are samosas and pastries, and homemade chocolate-chip cookies."

Alfie made a dive for Keira's bag at once. Keira's parents ran the Sleepy Gull Café on the clifftop, and everyone knew their food was the best in the whole of Savara.

"Alfie, don't grab like that," scolded Natasha. "You're a prince, not a puppy."

Keira giggled. "It's all right! My mum and dad sent plenty."

"That's lucky with Alfie around," Bea joked, giving her little brother a nudge.

After finishing the picnic, Bea and Keira walked down to the shore. They were wearing swimming costumes under their clothes, so they pulled off their shorts and T-shirts and jumped straight into the warm water. The sea made a gentle shooshing noise as it rolled on to the sand. Bea leaped over each wave, splashing water everywhere. Then the girls dived right in, pretending they were mermaids as they swam through the shallows.

"Nancy!" Bea called up the beach. "Can we go to Silver Rock Bay and look at the caves?"

Silver Rock Bay was a smaller cove just round the corner from the main beach. The sand there was a beautiful pale colour and there were exciting caves to explore. Bea had been allowed to play there before, as both she and Keira were strong swimmers and had passed their grade three life-saving certificate.

The cove could only be reached at low tide when the water rolled back, leaving room to walk past the rocky headland.

"Yes, you can, Princess Bea," Nancy called back. "But please be sensible."

Bea and Keira put their shorts and T-shirts back on and walked round the rocky headland. The seagulls wheeled over their heads. Little tufts of yellow and orange flowers bloomed on the cliff face.

The girls rounded the corner into Silver Rock Bay. Pink-and-white shells were strewn across the gleaming sand. Rows of dark caves lined the back of the beach and round the edge were the silvery rocks that gave the bay its name.

"Look at those shells!" cried Bea. "I've never seen so many pretty ones."

"They're lovely!" Keira picked up a

curly shell and held it to her ear. "I can hear the sea!"

Keira and Bea played in the waves for a while before exploring the largest cave at the back of the beach. It was dark and cool inside, and when they called loudly it made a brilliant echo. The girls climbed over the rocks at the cave entrance, looking into the rock pools for little crabs and tiny fish.

"We'd better go back," Keira said after a while. "We don't want to get trapped in the bay once the tide comes in."

They walked back to the shore. The breeze had grown stronger and the sea was dotted with thousands of tiny white-flecked waves.

Bea shaded her eyes and stared at the far end of the beach. "What's that funny shape? Do you think someone left their picnic bag behind?" She pointed to a little white blob on the rocks.

Keira frowned. "I think it moved!"

Bea started running, calling over her shoulder, "I'm going to see!" She sped across the sand, slowing down as she drew closer to the shape. Keira ran after her.'

The shape was curved and covered with downy-white fur as soft as a cloud. Bea's stomach swooped with excitement. "It's a little seal pup! But what's it doing here all alone?"

"My dad says baby seals feed on their mother's milk," Keira told her. "But after a few weeks the mother goes back out to sea. Then the pup follows her later."

"But seal families usually gather

together on the same beach, so why is this pup the only one here?" Bea knelt down on the sand and the seal pup turned its big black eyes on her. Lifting its whiskery nose, it gave a tiny little yelp.

"Oh, poor thing!" Keira crouched beside Bea. "Do you think it's waiting for its mother to come back?"

"I guess so." Bea touched the pup's snow-white fur. He was the softest, most beautiful animal she'd ever seen.

"Your dad told you not to even pick up anything furry," Keira reminded her.

"I know." Bea sighed. "But this baby seal is much too small to be here by himself. I wish I knew how to help."

Just then, Nancy appeared round the rocky headland leading back to the main beach. Waving her arms, she shouted, "Princess Bea! Keira! The tide's coming in and Prince Alfie's banged his knee."

"We'd better go!" Bea pulled a face. "Bye, little seal pup."

The baby seal pulled himself forward with his flippers. Sliding into a shallow rock pool, he lay there splashing and yelping happily. The girls laughed.

Then, reluctantly, they hurried across the beach and back round the headland.

Bea looked back as she turned the corner. She could just make out the furry white shape beside the rocks. She wished more than anything that she didn't have to leave the baby seal pup all alone.

Chapter Two

HMS
Bouncing Barnacle

The following morning, King George decided to take Bea, Natasha and Alfie on a boat trip.

They walked down to the harbour and climbed aboard the royal boat – HMS *Bouncing Barnacle*. Bea fizzed with excitement as she walked down the gangplank to the wooden deck.

"Where are we going today, Dad?" asked Natasha.

King George, who was dressed in his navy sailing suit and cap, untied the mooring rope. "We're going to visit somewhere very special called Nala Island."

"Ooh, an island!" Alfie's eyes lit up. "Is it special because there's buried treasure? We could pretend we're on a pirate ship and we've returned to the island to get our gold."

"No, there's no treasure, but there's lots of wildlife at this time of year and that's why it's such an extraordinary place." King George didn't notice Alfie's disappointed pout. He pulled in the gangplank, stowing it safely on the deck. "Let's raise the anchor and go!"

Mrs Stickler, the palace housekeeper, left the picnic basket in the cabin before handing round orange life jackets. Then the *Bouncing Barnacle* glided smoothly out of Savara Harbour. The king turned the wheel, guiding the boat towards a small rocky shape in the distance.

The *Bouncing Barnacle* had a powerful engine and sometimes Bea felt as though they were flying across the water. Natasha liked to sit inside at the small cabin table, but Bea preferred perching at the front to watch the prow of the boat cutting through the water and throwing up sparkling rainbow spray.

The *Bouncing Barnacle* slowed down as they drew closer to Nala Island. Bea leaned over the prow to gaze at the clear turquoise water. Shoals of little silver fish swam away from the approaching ship and the fronds of scarlet sea anemones swayed gently.

A wide sandy beach came into view with a tall cliff behind it dotted with nesting seabirds. Bea stared at a cluster of grey-and-white shapes lying on the sand. "Look!" she burst out. "Seals with their pups!"

King George smiled. "At this time of year the Nala beaches are full of seals and their young. It's quiet here and there are plenty of fish to eat when they return to the sea."

Their dad carried on explaining how the seals made their home on Nala Island, but Bea wasn't listening. She twisted round, looking back towards Savara. Next to the main beach was Silver Rock Bay where she'd found the seal pup the day before. She wondered whether the baby seal was all right and if his mother had come back to find him.

King George switched off the engine and they glided quietly towards the island. "We mustn't disturb the young seals and their mothers," he explained. "So we won't take the boat any closer, but you can swim right here if you like!"

Alfie gave a cheer. Then he pulled
off his life jacket and shorts, leaving
just his swimming trunks, and jumped
in. Natasha took off her life jacket and
climbed sedately down the ladder.

"Now listen, Beatrice," the king
added. "Don't get any ideas about
bringing a seal back to the palace."

"No, Dad!" Bea thought of the seal
pup she'd found the day before. She
had really wanted to take him home,
but perhaps his mother had come back
for him. She dipped her toes into the
warm water before sliding in.
At once a grey whiskery
face popped up close
by. The seal watched
Bea curiously for a
moment before diving
below the water.

"Look at me!" Alfie called. "I'm swimming with the seals."

"Shh, Alfie!" Natasha said, paddling up to her brother. "We're not meant to disturb the ones on the beach, remember?"

Bea loved the way the seals twisted

and turned, pulling themselves along with their powerful flippers. When they bobbed up to the surface the sunlight gleamed on their silky coats. The beach beyond was full of furry white seal pups. Bea smiled as she listened to their yelps and the deeper barking replies of the mother seals.

"Come back now, children. It's lunchtime," called Mrs Stickler sharply.

Bea swam reluctantly back to the boat, climbed up the ladder on to the deck and wrapped a towel round herself. A growling engine noise started up just as she took a cheese-and-ham roll from the picnic basket.

"What on earth is that?" King George looked up in surprise. "Boats shouldn't be fishing this close to the island."

Bea ran to the bow and saw a small red boat chugging into view. It sailed right up to the nearby beach and two men jumped out carrying fishing rods. The larger seals began barking loudly and some of the seal pups wriggled away in alarm.

"They're scaring the pups!" cried Bea.

"They shouldn't have landed there at

all." King George frowned. "The rule is: keep away from mother seals with their young because they shouldn't be disturbed. Stay here, children. I shall go and speak to them." He unloaded the inflatable dinghy and set off for the shore.

"Honestly! I thought everyone knew you shouldn't disturb the wildlife here," said Natasha. "It's an important nature reserve. Pass the cookies please, Bea."

"Maybe Dad's going to arrest them!" said Alfie, his eyes big and round.

"That's enough silliness," said Mrs Stickler.

King George spoke to the men on the shore and they set off in their boat again. When the king returned to the *Bouncing Barnacle* everyone carried on enjoying their lunch, except for Bea, who

studied the beach worriedly. Each of the
baby seals had returned to their mother
except for a tiny one that sat forlornly
by the water's edge. Was he lost? What
would happen when the tide came in if
he wasn't ready to swim?

Bea suddenly wondered if the same
thing had happened to the seal pup she'd
found the day before. Maybe he wasn't
meant to be in Silver Rock Bay at all.
Maybe he'd been swept away from his
real home. "Dad, can I talk to you about
something?" she asked.

King George was pouring himself a
cup of tea from a flask. "I really must
arrange for some signs to go on that
island," he said to Mrs Stickler. "Then
everyone will understand that landing
on those beaches is not allowed."

"That's a good idea, Sire," Mrs

Stickler replied. "People are very thoughtless at times."

"Dad?" Bea tried again. "I saw something yesterday and I think you should know…"

"Just a minute, Beatrice. I'm talking to Mrs Stickler," her dad said. "Now, what do you think the signs should say?"

Bea huffed a little and leaned over the side to splash her fingers in the water. There was no point trying to get her dad's attention when he was busy thinking about something else.

The seal pup beside the water's edge moved back up the beach again. Bea watched in relief as the little pup stopped beside a large grey seal and cuddled into her side.

King George started the engine and steered the *Bouncing Barnacle* back towards the mainland. Bea stared over at Silver Rock Bay as they crossed the waves. The bay was easy to make out with its row of dark caves at the bottom of the cliff, but she couldn't see the baby seal any more. Was he still there or had he found the strength to swim away? He could be camouflaged against the silvery white rocks.

Bea held the side of the boat tightly as they bounced through the waves. She needed to know that the seal pup was all right. As soon as they landed, she would go to find out.

Chapter Three

A Fish or Three

Bea wanted to hurry over to Silver Rock Bay the moment they drew up to the harbour side, but Mrs Stickler wouldn't let her go. She seemed to have an extra sense for when Bea was about to dash off somewhere.

"Please take this, Princess Beatrice." She handed Bea the picnic basket. "I need some help carrying everything back to the palace."

Bea tried not to pull a face as she took the basket handle. "Yes, Mrs Stickler."

The harbour was full of people washing the decks of their boats and mending their sails. The king waved to people cheerily as he went by. A row of stalls by the harbour wall were selling freshly caught fish. Soon the fishing boats would return to the sea to make their catches for the next day.

Bea trudged up the hill behind Natasha and Mrs Stickler. She wished she could escape to the beach. If she didn't go soon, the tide would come in and cut off Silver Rock Bay. Then it would be too late to check on the seal pup.

When they reached the palace, she left the picnic basket in the royal kitchen and hurried back to the front door, hoping for a chance to slip away.

"Princess Beatrice, I expect you need

a bath after all that swimming in the sea." Mrs Stickler stood at the palace entrance, blocking the way.

"Alfie should go first!" Bea said quickly.

"All right then." The housekeeper marched over to the stairs, calling, "Prince Alfred! Where are you?"

As soon as Mrs Stickler disappeared upstairs, Bea dashed to the back door. She ran through the palace garden and raced all the way down the hill to Savara, stopping to catch her breath as she reached the seafront.

The beach was empty. A strong breeze blew in from the sea, sending a piece of seaweed dancing across the sand. Bea took off her sandals and raced to the water's edge. Splashing through the rock pools, she hurried round the headland into Silver Rock Bay.

Far away across the sand, she spotted a little white shape lying between two rocks. The seal pup hadn't moved very far since the day before and there was no sign of his mother.

Bea ran to him and knelt down on the sand, gently stroking his fluffy white coat. The seal lifted his head a little and gave a tiny yelp. His eyes looked duller than before and Bea frowned. "You poor thing! I'm sure it's not right that you're here all alone."

"Bea!" A hand tapped Bea's shoulder and she jumped.

"Keira!" Bea scrambled up. "I didn't know you were going to be here."

Keira grinned. "I wanted to check that the seal pup was all right. We must have had the same idea!"

Bea nodded. "We went out on the boat this morning and I couldn't stop thinking about him." She told Keira about the trip to Nala Island and the men with the red boat who had disturbed the baby seals on the beach. "So maybe something like that happened to *our* seal too. Maybe he's not really meant to be here."

"That makes sense!" Keira pushed her ponytail over her shoulder. "But why isn't his mother looking for him? He must need her milk."

Bea climbed on to the rocks and
shaded her eyes as she looked out to sea.
"I don't know, but I can't see any seals
nearby."

Keira scrambled up beside her and
together they gazed at the water. Bea
kept hoping that a grey seal's head
would pop up above the surface but
nothing happened.

"Maybe the little pup will go back
to the sea to find his family," suggested
Keira doubtfully.

"I don't know how he can when he
looks so weak." Bea rubbed her forehead.
"We have to help him. If his mother
hasn't come back, we'll have to bring
him some fish to eat."

"That's a great idea!" Keira's eyes
lit up. "We have lots of fish back at the
café."

"Let's go to the harbour – it's even closer." Bea jumped down from the rocks and took some coins from her pocket. "I still have some pocket money I can spend."

The girls stroked the seal pup before running back along the beach. They stopped, panting, when they reached the harbour. The fish sellers were starting to pack up their stalls. Sailors were shaking out their nets and sweeping the decks of their boats.

"What kind of fish do seals like?" Bea whispered to Keira.

"I don't know!" Keira pulled a face. "Maybe some tuna … or cod or sardines?"

"Let's get all of them." Bea marched over to a fair-haired woman sitting behind the nearest stall. "Excuse me!

Could we buy some tuna, cod and sardines, please?"

"Of course!" The woman smiled and put some white fish on her weighing scales. "How much would you like of each?"

"Er, I'm not sure." Bea frowned. "Just a little bit I suppose. This is how much money I have." She showed the woman a handful of coins.

The fish seller looked surprised. "All right then! I'll parcel them up for you." She weighed the three pieces of fish and wrapped them up in paper.

"Thank you!" said Bea, taking the parcels of fish. The girls hurried along the harbourside, nearly bumping into Douglas, a fisherman with a white beard and wrinkled face who Bea knew very well. Douglas drove the royal boat from time to time when the king wanted some help. He had taken the royal family on many trips along the coast.

"Hello, Princess Bea." Douglas smiled. "You seem in an awful hurry."

"We're helping a little seal pup. He's ever so small and cute." Bea smiled back. "Are you going out to sea to catch more fish soon?"

"Not today. There's a storm coming." The fisherman nodded at the sky, where dark clouds were thickening. "No point in risking the boat when the sea is rough."

Bea and Keira exchanged worried looks. A gust of wind blew across the harbour, making the ships' sails flutter.

"We should hurry," Bea said to Keira. "The tide gets higher when there's a storm. Bye, Douglas! See you soon."

The girls rushed down the harbour steps and along the shore. The wind whipped up little whirlpools of sand on the empty beach. Bea ran faster, the fish parcels tucked under her arm. She and Keira raced around the headland as a cluster of storm clouds swarmed across the grey sky.

Chapter Four
Danger on the Shore

Bea spotted the enormous gulls as soon as she and Keira reached Silver Rock Bay. There were three of them strutting along the sand and squawking to each other. Bea glanced at the smaller seabirds nesting on the cliffs. These gulls were bigger and meaner with white bodies and black wings. They stalked towards the baby seal with a nasty look in their eyes.

"The seal pup!" cried Keira, and she and Bea began to run.

One of the gulls hopped on to a rock beside the seal. Tilting its head, it leaned towards the pup.

"Shoo!" Bea yelled, waving her arms frantically.

"Hey!" Keira joined in, flapping her arms too. "Get away from that seal."

The three gulls flew into the air before landing a little way off. They carried on strutting up and down the sand, watching the girls with their beady yellow eyes.

Bea stopped beside the seal pup, her heart pounding. "Those horrible birds! I don't trust them at all."

"Let's try giving him the fish," Keira said breathlessly. "If he gets stronger, he'll be able to swim away into the sea."

Bea knelt down and unwrapped the first parcel. "Here you are. Are you hungry?" She held out the tuna, the smell of raw fish filling her nose.

The pup sniffed at the fish, his whiskers twitching. Bea waited hopefully for him to take a bite but his head sank on to the sand again.

"Maybe he likes a different kind of fish." Keira unwrapped the next parcel and offered the pup the sardines.

This time the seal hardly lifted his head at all. When Bea put the parcel of cod beside him, he ignored that too.

Bea laid all the fish aside. "What's wrong, little seal?" She rubbed his soft white fur. "Don't you want any fish? You have to eat if you're going to get stronger."

"Maybe he's too young and he really needs milk," said Keira.

"We have to do something!" Bea glanced at the gulls prowling nearby. "As soon as we leave, those horrible birds will be back."

"We could move him into that big cave," Keira suggested. "I've never seen any gulls go in there."

Bea frowned. She wasn't sure if a dark cave would be scary for the seal pup but they had to get him away from the huge seagulls. "At least if his mother comes back, she'll still be able to find him."

Keira pulled off her jumper. "Let's wrap him in this and carry him over."

They laid the jumper on the sand and,

after a lot of pushing and tugging, they managed to slide the seal pup on to it. The little animal opened his black eyes wide and stared at the girls in surprise.

"It's all right! We're going to take care of you." Bea lifted the seal into her arms, smearing sand all over her T-shirt and Keira's jumper.

The pup felt heavy and Keira had to help by holding up his round tummy. He began to squirm as they carried him up the beach, wriggling his tail and flippers. His whiskers shook and he twitched his nose as if he was about to sneeze.

Bea held the seal pup tight as he began to yelp. "Don't be scared! We're only taking you to the cave. You'll be safer there!"

"Let's lay him on that sandbank." Keira nodded at a ridge of sand at the back of the cave. "He'll be tucked out of the way but he'll still be able to see the ocean."

Bea's arms began to ache and her foot slipped a little on a wet rock.

"Bea, are you all right?" Keira dived forward, holding the seal under his tummy.

"Don't worry – I'm fine." Steadying herself, Bea carried the baby seal the last few steps and, removing Keira's jumper from around his tummy, she set him down gently on the sand.

Cool air drifted through the cave and water dripped down the smooth walls. The baby seal wriggled and sniffed the air before laying his head on the sand as if he was tired from all the excitement.

Bea knelt down beside the seal pup. "I promise we'll come back to check on you tomorrow." She swallowed. Tomorrow seemed such a long way off.

What if the seal pup needed her before then?

Keira stroked the seal's head. "Look at his big dark eyes! I think he's the cutest thing I've ever seen."

The pup gave a long mew and twitched his whiskers.

Bea laughed. "I think he agrees with you! He's certainly the furriest creature I've ever met. I guess he needs all that fluff to keep out the cold sea wind."

"We should think of a name for him," Keira said suddenly. "How about Snowy because of his lovely snow-white fur?"

"Snowy suits him!" Bea grinned, but then her smile faded. "I know he's safer here, but I wish we didn't have to leave him!"

"I want to stay too." Keira looked out of the cave entrance. "But the tide's really coming in now, so we'd better go!"

Bea gave Snowy one last stroke before she and Keira hurried out of the cave. The sea poured into the bay, washing away their footprints from the sand. The nasty-looking gulls croaked to each other and flapped away over the cliffs. The wind grew fiercer, turning the waves into mounds of white foam.

Keira and Bea raced round the headland just as the tide reached the rocks. Savara Beach was empty with just a few sandcastles scattered across the shore.

"Everyone's gone home early," said Keira.

Bea glanced at the dark clouds marching across the sky. "I guess they didn't want to be caught in the storm. The sea looks rough already."

"At least Snowy will stay safe and dry in the cave." Keira shook the sand off her jumper and put it back on.

The wind surged across the seafront, shaking the palm trees. Bea said goodbye to Keira. Then she headed for home, struggling up the hill against the rising wind. She hoped the seal's mother would come back to find her pup. The little animal certainly needed someone to look after him.

Chapter Five
The Moonlit Cave

The sky grew darker and the wind whistled round the palace all the way through dinner that evening. Bea tried not to worry about the seal pup as she ate her chicken pie and carrots. Luckily, no one had noticed she'd left Ruby Palace earlier that afternoon, though Mrs Stickler had asked her sharply whether she'd had her bath yet.

Heavy rain was pouring down by the

time Bea got changed for bed. She put
on her paw-print pyjamas and sat on the
window sill, watching puddles growing
on the palace drive and water dripping
from the lemon trees in the orchard.

There were thumping footsteps outside the door and Alfie burst in. "I'll never sleep if there's thunder and lightning. It's too exciting!"

Bea smiled. She didn't mind Alfie rushing in like a brother-shaped tornado. At least he was stopping her from worrying about the seal pup. "Maybe there won't be much thunder this time."

Natasha appeared in the doorway in her gold satin pyjamas, her hair neatly brushed. "Mrs Stickler says you should both be in bed – especially you, Alfie."

"We were just talking about how bad the storm might be," said Bea.

"The worst weather won't arrive till tomorrow morning," Natasha told them. "Mrs S looked up the weather forecast."

Bea's heart lifted. Maybe there would be another chance to check on Snowy before the storm arrived.

"It's a good thing we had our day at the beach yesterday," Natasha went on. "Nancy says those caves you went in get flooded every time there's a storm. There'll be water everywhere!"

Bea stared at her sister. "You mean the ones in Silver Rock Bay? But the shoreline is a long way from the caves."

"I know but that's what Nancy told me," Natasha insisted. "She remembers how deeply they flooded in the last storm. Come on, Alfie. It really *is* bedtime!"

Alfie followed Natasha, grumbling loudly.

Bea paced up and down her bedroom, her heart racing. She and Keira hadn't kept the baby seal safe after all. She pictured Snowy looking confused as the

sea flooded into the cave – filling the
rock pools and covering the sand. She
had to rescue him before the water got
that far! But it was dark outside … and
there was no chance of even reaching
Silver Rock Bay until low tide.

She sank on to the window sill again,
frowning at the raindrops sliding down
the glass. Natasha had said the storm
wouldn't reach the shore till morning.
Maybe she could leave the palace very
early tomorrow and move the seal before
the storm reached the cave.

Bea ran down to the palace kitchen
and read the list of tide times pinned
to the wall. The tide would be low by
five o'clock. If she went then, she would
reach the cove safely. Maybe she could
fetch the seal and bring him back to the
palace. Her dad would be cross, but at

least the pup would be safe.

Hurrying back to her room, she set her alarm clock for five before climbing into bed. In just a few hours she would begin her rescue plan.

Bea kept dreaming of caves and seals, then waking up to check the time. When her alarm went at five o'clock she jumped out of bed and pulled on trousers and a T-shirt. Then she took a torch from her drawer. There was still an hour or two till sunrise and she would need the light to see her way along the shore.

Tiptoeing downstairs, she grabbed her raincoat and raced to the orchard. She climbed the plum tree that grew next to the palace wall, before jumping to the other side. Then she hurried down the hill into Savara.

A fierce wind swept along the seafront
and Bea shivered under her raincoat.
It was strange seeing the streets so
empty. The moon peeped between the
storm clouds, turning the puddles on
the pavement silver. The branches of the
palm trees waved in the wind like the
arms of angry monsters.

Bea raced down the sandy beach
with the roar of the ocean filling her
ears. Waves were crashing against the
cliff, sending spray flying into the air.
As she reached the headland a jagged
white line flashed across the distant sky
followed by a growl of thunder. Bea
caught her breath. The storm was still
out at sea but it was getting closer. She
shone the torch on to the pale sand,
picking her way round the rock pools.

"Snowy? Are you all right?" Bea

hurried to the mouth of the cave, her feet slipping on the wet stones.

Another lightning flash broke from the dark sky. Then blackness settled over everywhere again.

Bea shone her torch into the cave and found Snowy exactly where she and Keira had left him. She crouched beside the seal pup and stroked his soft head. She wished Keira was here helping her again. Moving the creature by herself wasn't going to be easy.

Snowy yelped as thunder rolled across the bay.

"Shh! Don't worry – I'm going to look after you," Bea whispered, rubbing his furry coat.

The moon came out again, casting bright flecks across the wild sea. Bea frowned. The water was higher than it should be at low tide and the thunder was growing louder too. If the storm was approaching, there was no time to lose.

Bea stuck her torch in her pocket and laid her raincoat on the sand beside the

little seal. As she gently pushed him
on to it Snowy began to wriggle and
squeak. Bea picked him up, all wrapped
in the raincoat, and stumbled out of the
cave mouth just as lightning flashed
through the sky once
more. This time the
thunder came faster
and the seal hid his
face under Bea's arm.

Bea stumbled
across the beach and
round the headland,
clutching Snowy
tightly. By the time she
reached the seafront with
its row of palm trees, her
arms ached. She sank
on to the steps of the
promenade and laid the

seal pup on her lap. The little animal was so heavy. How was she going to get him all the way to the palace?

She rose to her feet and lifted him up once again. As she stumbled past the harbour, lightning flashed and the clouds broke open in a sudden fierce downpour. Bea spotted the *Bouncing Barnacle* bobbing in the harbour. Maybe she could shelter in the royal boat for a while?

She crossed the gangplank slowly, careful not to lose her balance on the slippery walkway. Then she tried the cabin door, sighing with relief when she found it was unlocked. She laid Snowy gently across the cabin seat. Then she slammed the door, shutting out the growling storm.

Chapter Six
A Chance
for Snowy

The storm swirled around the harbour, rocking the boats moored to the quayside. Bea held on to the window ledge as HMS *Bouncing Barnacle* lurched from side to side. She watched the waves curl over like huge white claws and smash into the harbour wall. The rain beat faster against the roof of the little cabin.

Bea took a deep breath. She couldn't

remember a storm as bad as this one, but she and the seal pup were tucked away safely. Surely the harbour walls would keep out the worst of the wind and the waves?

Lightning flashed right overhead, followed by a gigantic boom of thunder. Bea looked at Snowy in alarm but the pup had closed his eyes. The storm marched in from the sea and each time lightning flashed the harbour lit up for a few seconds. Bea caught her breath as a loose fishing net blew past and disappeared into the rainy darkness.

At last the storm slowed to a gentle patter of raindrops. The angry black clouds blew past, giving way to dull grey ones and the roar of the wind faded. A tiny glimmer of dawn peeped between the clouds but the seal pup still didn't open his eyes. Bea waited until the boat stopped rocking so fiercely. Then she opened the cabin door quietly, careful not to wake the baby seal.

Water glistened on the deck of the boat and the quayside was covered with puddles. Bea spotted a small figure with a dark ponytail running past the harbour. "Keira!" she shouted. "Over here!"

Keira spun round and Bea waved wildly. "It's all right," she called as Keira came closer. "I've got Snowy here – he's safe."

Keira hurried across the gangplank. "What happened?" she panted, her eyes widening as she saw the seal pup lying on the cabin seat.

Bea explained that the caves usually flooded when there was a storm. "So I *had* to move him … but I didn't get very far. He's so heavy!"

She stroked Snowy's furry head. The seal pup opened his eyes and watched the girls quietly.

"The storm was awful!" Keira crouched down next to Bea and Snowy. "Did you see all that lightning?"

"It was quite scary when the thunder got louder," Bea admitted.

"You're really brave being here all alone in the storm," said Keira. "No wonder Snowy is so quiet. It must have scared him."

Bea frowned worriedly. Snowy was lying very still and his eyes looked dull. "It's more than that," she said at last. "I think he's getting weaker. Look how he hardly lifts his head any more."

Keira gently rubbed the seal's coat. "There must be something we can do to help. Maybe he's cold. We could wrap him up in blankets..."

Bea shook her head. "I don't think that'll help." Sitting down beside him,

she drew the seal pup on to her lap.
His head flopped and his flippers hung
loosely by his side. Bea tried stroking
his cheek but Snowy just closed his eyes
again.

The next burst of lightning was just
a distant flicker. Then a faint rumble of
thunder like a giant's snore came from
further inland.

"At least the storm has passed now,"
said Keira. "Shall I hold him for a
minute?"

Bea carefully passed the seal to Keira
before pacing up and down the little
cabin. "I think Snowy needs to be back
where he belongs with the other seals.
He needs his mum to look after him."

"But we don't even know where he
comes from," said Keira.

"Nala Island has more seals than

anywhere else I know and it's close by too. I'm sure Snowy must have come from there." Bea went to the little cabin window and stared at the frothy grey ocean.

The waves outside the harbour were whipped up high by the wind, but they weren't crashing against the sea wall as fiercely as before. Tiny glints of daylight were peeping through the grey clouds.

"How are we supposed to get Snowy to Nala Island?" Keira stared at her friend. "Bea, you're not going to do something wild are you?"

"We have to find a way to get there," Bea said firmly. "If we don't get Snowy back to his mum soon, it could be too late." A lump rose in her throat and she swallowed it quickly.

Keira gazed at the seal pup. "You're

right! But we can't take the boat out on our own."

Bea bit her lip, trying hard to think. Then she noticed a light in the cabin of one of the boats nearby. "We're not the only ones here! Maybe we can get someone to help us." She dashed on to the deck, nearly slipping on the gangplank as she rushed over to the other boat.

"Excuse me! Can you help us?"

Douglas opened the cabin door and looked at Bea in surprise.

"What are you doing

here, Princess Bea? Shouldn't you be safe and sound at the palace?"

Bea quickly explained about the seal pup and how she'd moved him out of the cave. "Now we've got to get him back to Nala Island. He's getting so weak."

"I see!" Douglas scratched his beard.

"So I need someone to take us there and you've driven the *Bouncing Barnacle* loads of times," Bea went on hopefully. "You will help us, won't you?"

The fisherman frowned thoughtfully. "I know a good route to Nala Island. I can have you there and back before you blink!" He smiled. "Now let me take a look at this little seal."

Bea took him back to the royal boat. Douglas put the keys into the ignition and the engine roared. Bea went to the cupboard and found life jackets for them all.

Keira struggled into her life jacket. "Snowy, wake up!" She crouched beside the seal pup. "I think he's getting weaker."

Bea could see the animal's tummy moving as he breathed but his eyes stayed shut. "Poor Snowy! We'd better hurry."

Hurrying down the gangplank, she undid the rope on the quayside. Then Keira helped her pull in the wooden gangway and lay it on the deck.

"Are you ready?" asked Douglas. "The sea will feel quite rough."

"We're ready!" Bea said firmly.

Douglas manoeuvred the boat forward, heading for the narrow gap in the harbour wall. The *Bouncing Barnacle* rocked uneasily and then,

Suddenly, they were through the harbour entrance and out on the open sea.

Chapter Seven

Storm Waves

The *Bouncing Barnacle* dipped and lurched. Waves slapped against the sides of the boat, sending torrents of spray into the air. Bea gripped the table, trying to keep her balance. Keira gave a shriek as the boat rocked sharply again, tipping her on to the cabin floor.

"Are you all right?" Bea called.

"I'm fine!" gasped Keira. "I just feel a little seasick."

"Don't worry – I'll look after Snowy."
Bea knelt down and wrapped her arms
round the seal pup.

As they sailed on the sky lightened
and the sea grew calmer. Bea peered into
the distance. Shouldn't they be able to
see the island's rocky outline by now?
It was hard to tell where the grey sky
ended and the grey sea began. The lights
of Savara had faded behind them and
the jagged waves seemed to stretch on
forever.

"How long till we reach the island?"
she asked Douglas.

"We'll be there soon. It's taken a little
longer because the wind is so strong,"
the fisherman replied. "How is your seal
pup?"

"I think he's getting weaker." Bea
stroked Snowy softly and stared through

the window, hoping to see Nala Island. She thought she saw a rocky cliff but it turned out to be a patch of dark cloud.

Suddenly she remembered the binoculars in the cupboard. "I know something that might help us." Clutching Snowy tightly, she took the binoculars from a hook inside the door. Then she hurried to the prow of the boat and lifted them to her eyes.

Nala Island appeared in the distance, almost hidden by greyish mist. Bea's stomach swooped with excitement as the island grew bigger through the glasses. "It's all right – I can see it now! It's right there."

She went back to the cabin and passed the binoculars to Douglas. The old fisherman peered through them, before steering left a little and pushing the lever to increase the speed. The boat sprang forward, riding the highs and lows of the waves. Sea spray flew high into the air, hitting the cabin roof and trickling down the window.

Little by little the island became clearer. Its rough cliffs, dotted with grass and pink sea thrift, jutted out against the gloomy sky. Bea spotted the grey seals with their tiny white pups lying on the pale sand. The air was filled with barking seal calls and the cries of the seabirds nesting among the rocks.

Douglas pulled the lever back to slow the boat down. Then he switched off the engine a short way from the beach and lowered the anchor, just as Bea's dad had done the day before. The seal pup lifted his head and gave a faint whine.

"I think he can hear the other seals," said Keira.

Bea smiled. "That's right, Snowy. You're nearly home."

"But how do we get him to the beach?" asked Keira. "The sea looks really rough and I don't even have a swimming costume."

"We can use the inflatable dinghy." Bea rushed out on to the deck and pulled the toggle to inflate the little orange boat. Together she and Keira carried the seal pup over and laid him in the bottom of the inflatable.

Douglas helped Bea to use the rope pulley to lower Keira and the seal pup on to the water. Then Bea climbed down the ladder into the boat.

"See you soon, girls. Good luck!" said Douglas.

The girls waved at him, before taking
their oars and starting to paddle.
The wind whistled around the island,
whipping the waves up high.

"It doesn't feel like we're getting any
closer!" Keira called over the whoosh of
the waves.

Bea glanced at the shore. They had
rowed for a while but the beach still
seemed a long way away. "We have to
keep going! It's sure to get easier, right?"

A tall wave slapped the inflatable,
filling the bottom with water. The seal
pup gave a tiny yelp. Bea scooped the
water out as best she could and dug her
paddle into the sea again. What if the
rough waves tipped the inflatable over?
She and Keira had life jackets but the
seal pup might be too weak to swim.

At last the waves grew calmer as they

came closer to the shore. The current pushed them towards a row of dark rocks at the end of the beach. Bea jumped from the boat and waded through the warm water, pulling the inflatable towards the shore.

Keira jumped out too and helped to hold the boat steady. "Don't you think we should land closer to the other seals?"

"No, we might scare them," said Bea. "My dad says you should always keep away from mother seals and their babies so you don't disturb them."

The bottom of the inflatable bumped against the sand and Bea started hauling it out of the shallows.

"Bea, wait!" Keira wiped the sea spray out of her eyes. "If we don't get closer, how will Snowy ever find his mum? He's much too weak to get across the beach by himself."

Bea looked at the exhausted seal pup lying in the orange dinghy. She knew Keira was right. The beach stretched a long way and Snowy's mother would never hear him over the barking of the other seals unless he was closer. "It's just that the inflatable is so big and bright... Maybe we can sneak him closer by lifting him out of the boat and carrying him through the water."

The girls took off their life jackets and left them inside the inflatable, which they pulled up on to the sand beside the rocks. Then they lifted Snowy back into the shallows, holding him carefully under his tummy. The seal pup seemed to enjoy the water, swishing his flippers weakly.

"It's all right, Snowy! We're almost

there now." Bea stroked his white fur and excitement fizzed inside her. Soon Snowy would be back with the other seals again. She hoped with all her heart that his mother would be there to meet him!

Chapter Eight

Snowy Comes Home

Bea and Keira waded through the sea, holding Snowy tightly. The water came up to their waists and now and then a wave slapped against them.

The seal pup dipped his nose in the water and gave a soft yelp. Bea kept a determined grip on the little animal. Further along, the sand was full of grown-up seals and fluffy white pups. If they could get Snowy closer, he might be able find his mother again.

Gradually, the sea became shallower. "We should move really slowly," whispered Bea, "so that we don't scare the seals."

They waded forward slowly, trying to stay quiet until Keira suddenly fell over with a huge splash.

"Are you all right?" cried Bea.

"I'm fine! I just tripped over a rock under the water." Keira pulled a face as she got up. There was a large graze across her knee.

"We've got some plasters back on the *Bouncing Barnacle*. As soon as we get back, I'll find one for you." Bea struggled to hold on to Snowy as an extra-large wave crashed into them.

"I'll be OK. It doesn't hurt that much," Keira said bravely, but she limped when she tried to walk.

"You should wait here," Bea said. "I'll be ok. It's not much further."

"Thanks, Bea!" Keira kissed Snowy's fur. "Goodbye, Snowy! I'll never forget you."

Bea carried on wading through the

shallow water, holding Snowy tightly. The beach was full of large grey seals with their pups and, as she drew closer, the noise became deafening. At last, Bea stepped on to the sand. The seals close by looked at her in alarm.

Bea crept further up the beach and laid Snowy gently on the sand before darting behind some large rocks. She watched anxiously. What if Snowy's mother didn't hear him? What if she was out at sea hunting for fish?

The seal pups on the beach called for their mothers with long squeaky cries, but Snowy stayed quiet.

"Come on, Snowy!" whispered Bea. "You have to call out like the others."

At first Snowy didn't move. Then, at last, he lifted his head and gave a soft cry.

Bea peeked round the seaweed-covered rocks. If only Snowy would call louder like the other seal pups!

Snowy lifted his head again and gave a louder yelp. Then he gave two more cries before dropping his head on the sand in exhaustion.

Bea held her breath. Then, from further up the beach, came an answering bark.

A large grey seal came loping across the sand, barking loudly. Snowy's whiskers quivered and he gave another cry. The mother seal stopped, turning her head from side to side as she listened for the sound. Then she rushed up to Snowy and sniffed his snow-white fur.

Bea smiled widely as Snowy and his mum touched noses. She turned round to make a big thumbs-up signal to Keira, who grinned and waved back.

Snowy yelped once more and his mother gave an answering bark. Then the seal pup cuddled against his mother's side and closed his eyes. Bea's heart rose as she watched them settle down together on the sand. At last she tiptoed back into the shallows to meet Keira.

"You were right, Bea!" Keira beamed. "This was exactly the right place to bring Snowy."

"I'm really glad you were here with me." Bea took Keira's arm and helped her limp back to the inflatable.

The girls put on their life jackets and rowed back to the *Bouncing Barnacle*. The storm winds had quietened into a cheerful breeze and patches of blue sky peeped between the clouds. Bea grabbed the binoculars as soon as she was back on deck. She could just about make out the shape of Snowy and his mum still cuddled up on the sand.

Bea and Keira put away the inflatable dinghy while Douglas switched on the boat's engine. Then they lifted the anchor and the fisherman swung the wheel round, steering them back towards Savara.

The journey back was much quicker and, as they sailed into the harbour, the

sun came out from behind the clouds.
The quayside was empty except for a
small flock of seagulls sitting on the
harbour wall.

Bea smiled as Douglas gave back the
keys to the *Bouncing Barnacle*. "Thank
you for helping us. We really couldn't
have done it without you!" She hesitated.
"My dad doesn't exactly know about the
seal and…"

"That's all right," said the fisherman.
"I'll let you tell him when you're ready."

Bea nodded with relief. She
remembered how much her dad had
wanted to protect the island's seals from
noisy boats. Sometimes he showed that
he really was an animal lover after all.
"I will explain it all to him one day,"
she told Douglas, "and I think he'll be
happy that we saved Snowy."

Douglas nodded and gave her a crinkly-eyed smile.

The church clock chimed seven. The row of seagulls flapped into the air and flew off over the waves.

"I didn't realise it was still so early," said Keira. "It feels like we've been sailing for hours but it's not even breakfast time yet."

"I wish it was! I'm really hungry." Bea's stomach rumbled as she slid the gangplank into place.

"Maybe you could come to the Sleepy Gull Café for breakfast," suggested Keira. "There'll be sausages and hash browns, and lots of chocolate milk."

"Mmm, that sounds good." Bea closed the cabin door.

The girls waved goodbye to Douglas and made their way along the harbour.

They linked arms as they headed up
the hill towards the Sleepy Gull Café.
Stopping at the top of the cliff, they
gazed across the sea to Nala Island –
now just a tiny dot in the distance.

"I really hope we meet Snowy again
one day," said Keira.

"Me too!" Bea opened the café door
and breathed in the delicious cooking
smells inside. "Come on – I could eat a
mountain!"

Chapter Nine
Fun in the Waves

"Bea, where are you going with that picnic basket?" Natasha called across Savara Beach. "Come back! You're going to get the food wet."

Bea ran down to the water's edge and gazed out to sea. It had been three weeks since she and Keira had taken Snowy across to Nala Island to find his mother and Bea had thought about the seal pup every day. Had he grown a lot bigger since then? Maybe he had even learnt to swim! She kept hoping for a chance to see him but her father had been too busy to sail the *Bouncing Barnacle* over to the island.

"Bea, don't run off with the chocolate chip muffins," yelled Alfie.

Bea turned back, grinning. "Don't worry, I've only had three. Just kidding!" She let go as Alfie wrestled the basket from her hands.

"Alfie, don't be silly!" called Natasha. "What will people say if they see you behaving like that? I knew this picnic was a bad idea."

"At least it's a sunny day, Princess Natasha," said Nancy, who was following them with the picnic rug under her arm. "It's nice to see the sunshine after all the windy weather."

Bea spotted Keira coming down the cliff path. She ran to meet her friend while Natasha and Nancy spread out the picnic rug and Alfie stood guard over the basket of food. Keira had brought parcels of spring rolls and delicious pizza slices from the Sleepy Gull Café, and soon they were all settled on the rug with cups of lemonade and plates full of food.

Alfie jumped up first, his mouth full of chocolate chip muffin. "I'm going to build a sand fort with a moat."

"I'll help you, Prince Alfie." Nancy picked up a bucket and spade.

"Can we go round the corner to Silver Rock Bay?" Bea asked the maid. "The rock pools are so much better there."

"All right, Princess Bea," said Nancy. "Be sensible, won't you?"

Keira and Bea grabbed fishing nets and buckets, and raced round the headland into Silver Rock Bay. Bea ran straight to the place where they'd found the seal three weeks ago. She gazed at the little rock pool where the pup had first splashed and sighed deeply. "The place seems so empty without Snowy."

"I know!" said Keira. "I just wish we could see him one more time."

"At least we know he's happy now." Bea managed a smile. "Shall we see who can catch the most crabs?"

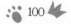

They fished in the rock pools for a while, catching tiny crabs and silvery fish and counting them before putting them back again. Then they took off their T-shirts and shorts and ran into the sea in their swimming costumes. The sun beamed down and the waves crashed on to the sand in a rush of white sea foam.

"Wahoo!" yelled Bea, jumping over one breaker after another.

Keira threw herself into the sea with a huge splash, splattering water all over Bea. Then they swam around in the shallows, letting each new wave take them for a ride.

"I suppose we should go back," Keira said at last. "We've been here for ages."

"Let's stay a few more minutes." Bea floated around on her back, her dark hair waving in the water like a sea anemone. "The sea is so warm today. It makes me wish I could live here forever like a seal!"

There was a squeaky bark close to her ear. Bea was so surprised that she lost her balance. Dipping below the surface, she came up spluttering. "What was that? Did you hear something?"

"Hear what?" Keira frowned. "Are you all right, Bea?"

"I'm sure I heard something…" Bea stared thoughtfully at the waves.

A moment later, a silky grey head popped up from below the surface. Two large black eyes watched her curiously and the seal twitched his dark whiskers before diving back below the water again. Then two more seal faces popped up a short distance away.

"Seals!" cried Keira. "They must be here looking for fish."

Bea spotted a smaller seal with patches of white fur across his grey coat. "Look, Keira! Do you think that's Snowy?"

Keira's face lit up. "It might be! He still has a few patches of baby fur."

"Snowy!" Bea called softly. "Is that you?"

The little seal dipped below the water, appearing in a different spot a second later. Then he swam right up to Bea and brushed against her. Bea stroked his silky coat, laughing as Snowy popped his nose out of the sea and shook the water off his whiskers.

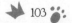

"Snowy, you came back to see us!"
cried Keira.

The seal barked softly and glided all
around them, flicking his tail. Bea dived
into the water and swam with the pup.
Keira joined in too, and they floated and
dived and flicked water over each other.

Bea stopped to catch her breath.
"You're such a good swimmer, Snowy!"

"I bet seals learn to swim really quickly," said Keira admiringly. "Look how graceful he is!"

The little seal popped up right beside Bea and Keira and gave a happy bark. Bea laughed and touched noses with him. Then the girls dived in and swam some more. Snowy zoomed all around, swishing his tail.

"Princess Bea! Keira! Time to go," Nancy called from the beach.

"Just five more minutes!" cried Bea.

"I'm afraid we have to go now," said Nancy. "Come on, girls!"

Bea touched noses with Snowy one more time. "Goodbye, Snowy! I hope you catch lots of fish. We promise to come back and see you again soon!"

The girls waded back to the shore and picked up their fishing nets. Bea turned round to wave as they left the bay and saw one last glimpse of a silky tail flicking above the water.

"Snowy looks really healthy and strong," said Keira. "I'm so happy we rescued him."

Bea smiled. "Me too! Helping animals is the best thing in the whole world."